THE HAUNTED KILLER MYSTERY

ALAQMAR VAKHARIA

Made with ♥ on the Notion Press Platform
www.notionpress.com

Contents

Acknowledgements   *v*

  1. The   1

  2. The Mission   4

  3. The   6

  4. The   8

Acknowledgements

I wanted to say thanks to everyone who helped me make this book from my brothers and my sister and notion press my brother and sister helped me alot. And notion press to help me launch this book to the world. Since i was a kid i wanted to write my own book i have written my book long ago it was just a biography about a famous youtuber and everyone showed me lot of support and helped me . I also wanted to say thanks to my freinds and my classmates for showing a lot of support and my last book has only 1 left in stock. Thank you everyone of making my passion my reality.Hope you have fun reading this book.
    THANK YOU!

CHAPTER ONE

The

The small town of Ravenswood was plagued by a string of mysterious disappearances. No one knew who or what was behind it, but the villagers were terrified. The local authorities were at a loss, and the villagers were left to fend for themselves.

One night, a group of friends decided to investigate the disappearances on their own. They had heard rumors of an old abandoned mansion on the outskirts of town, said to be haunted by the spirits of those who had gone missing.

The friends set out to the mansion, armed with nothing but their courage and a few flashlights. As they entered the dark, musty building, they immediately felt a sense of dread. The air was thick with the stench of death, and they could hear strange noises coming from the shadows.

As they made their way deeper into the mansion, they began to uncover clues. They found diary entries, old photographs, and other evidence that suggested that the disappearances were not the work of some supernatural force, but of a human killer.

The diary entries were written by the previous owner of the mansion, a wealthy businessman who had gone mad after his family died in a tragic accident. He had turned the mansion into a twisted laboratory, where he conducted gruesome experiments on the villagers he had kidnapped.

The old photograph they found was of the businessman and his family, taken before the accident. The photograph was torn and smudged with blood, adding an eerie feel to it.

As the friends were about to leave the mansion, they were ambushed by the businessman. He had been watching them the entire time, and had been waiting for the perfect moment to strike. He was wielding a cleaver and had a crazed look in his eyes.

The friends fought for their lives, but the businessman was stronger than they had anticipated. They were able to hold him off for a while, but he was able to critically injure one of the friends. In a desperate move, one of the friends managed to grab a nearby fireplace poker and strike the businessman on the head. But to their horror, the businessman didn't die, instead he ran away, leaving a trail of blood behind him.

The remaining friends managed to escape the mansion and ran back to the village to tell the authorities what they had discovered. The police arrived at the mansion and found the diary entries, the photograph, but no sign of the businessman's body.

The villagers were shocked to learn the truth behind the disappearances and were left in a constant state of fear, knowing that the businessman was still out there, possibly planning his next move. And the mansion remained abandoned, a dark and foreboding reminder of the horrors that had taken place within its walls. The friends and the villagers were always looking over their shoulder, never knowing when or where the businessman would strike next.

CHAPTER TWO

The mission

The villagers of Ravenswood lived in fear, knowing that the businessman was still at large. The police searched for him relentlessly, but he seemed to have vanished without a trace. The friends who had uncovered the truth about the disappearances were hailed as heroes, but they were haunted by their experience at the mansion.

As the days passed, the villagers began to notice strange occurrences around the town. Objects would go missing, and people reported seeing a man who matched the businessman's description lurking in the shadows. Some even claimed to have seen him in their homes at night.

The friends knew that the businessman was seeking revenge for their interference, and they were determined to stop him. They began to investigate the strange occurrences, and soon discovered that the businessman had not fled the town, but was hiding in plain sight.

He had taken on a new identity and was living among the villagers, waiting for the perfect moment to strike. The friends alerted the authorities, and together they set a trap for the businessman.

The trap was set using the latest technology, consisting of hidden cameras and alarms. The police also set up a decoy, making the businessman believe that they had found a new victim, and luring him into the trap.

The trap worked, and the businessman was finally caught. As he was being led away in handcuffs, the villagers breathed a sigh of relief. But their relief was short-lived, as they soon discovered that the businessman had not been working alone. The authorities searched for the accomplice, but they were unable to find any leads. It was as if the accomplice had vanished into thin air.

In the end, justice was served, but the villagers were left with a lingering sense of unease, knowing that the accomplice was still out there, and could potentially continue the businessman's twisted work.

CHAPTER THREE

The

The villagers of Ravenswood were still on edge, knowing that the businessman's accomplice was still at large. The police searched for the accomplice tirelessly, but they were unable to find any leads. The friends who had uncovered the truth about the disappearances also kept an eye out for any suspicious activity, but it seemed that the accomplice had truly vanished into thin air.

However, one day, they received a breakthrough. A person who matched the description of the accomplice was spotted in a nearby town. The police were immediately alerted and they rushed to the scene. The person was arrested, and upon further investigation, it was discovered that they had a connection to the businessman. They had worked in the same company and were seen together several times, which made the police think that they were the accomplice.

The villagers were relieved that they had finally caught the accomplice. But as the investigation progressed, it became clear that the person they had arrested was innocent. They had been falsely accused and had no involvement in the disappearances or the businessman's twisted experiments.

The real accomplice was still out there, and the villagers were left feeling even more uneasy than before.

The friends who had uncovered the truth about the disappearances felt guilty for falsely accusing an innocent person. They had been so focused on finding the accomplice that they had overlooked crucial evidence that would have cleared the person's name. The police also apologized for their mistake.

As the authorities were tearing down the mansion, they found a hidden room in the basement, where they discovered a clue that led them to the real accomplice. It was a journal, in which the businessman had detailed his plan and his accomplice's involvement in the crimes. It revealed that the accomplice was someone who was close to the businessman and had helped him in his twisted experiments.

The villagers were left in shock as they realized that the accomplice was someone they knew and trusted. The police immediately began a manhunt for the accomplice, but they were unable to find him. It was as if he had vanished into thin air.

The friends who had uncovered the truth were hailed as heroes, but they knew that they could never truly escape the horrors they had faced. They would always be haunted by the memory of the mansion, the evil that had lurked within its walls, the innocent man falsely accused and the fact that the real accomplice was still out there, free.

CHAPTER FOUR

The

villagers of Ravenswood were still on edge, knowing that the businessman's accomplice was still at large. The police searched for the accomplice tirelessly, but they were unable to find him. The friends who had uncovered the truth about the disappearances also kept an eye out for any suspicious activity, but it seemed that the accomplice had truly vanished into thin air.

However, one day, the police received a tip about the accomplice's whereabouts. They were told that he was hiding out in an old cabin deep in the woods. The police quickly assembled a team and set out to find the accomplice.

The friends who had uncovered the truth about the disappearances also joined the police in their search. They knew that they had to stop the accomplice before he could cause any more harm.

As they reached the cabin, they could hear noises coming from inside. The police carefully approached the cabin, weapons at the ready. They kicked down the door and rushed inside, but to their disappointment, the cabin was empty.

They searched the cabin thoroughly but found no sign of the accomplice. They did find a map that showed the accomplice's escape route and followed the trail. After hours of tracking, they finally caught sight of the accomplice, but he was able to evade capture by slipping into the dense forest.

But one of the freinds was fast enough to catch him and the police man arrived and sent him to jail

The friends who had uncovered the truth were hailed as heroes, but they knew that they could never truly escape the horrors they had faced. They would always be haunted by the memory of the mansion, the evil that had lurked within its walls, the innocent man falsely accused.

The end